I0721308

UNSEEN

(Tales from La Paz)

By

Gonzalo Araoz

To Mila, Mati, and Nico,

In memory of my parents, Luis Araoz Q. and

Mireya S. de Araoz,

who raised me in the city of La Paz.

Table of Contents

"Illimani" (2012).

500x100 cm. Acrylic on canvas (24 pieces) by

Gonzalo Araoz.

Photograph: Hugh Tuffen.

Enquiries: gonzalo.araoz.arts@gmail.com

Prologue

One does not arrive in El Alto.

One emerges.

As if from another life and into the mist—panting in the high, thin air, neither here nor there. The body, foreign to itself, reels.

It is not advisable to move, not yet. The coca leaf tea, bitter and green, is a quiet pact with the mountain gods—if they allow you breath, you may stay.

The terminal, at four thousand metres, is a not quite real place, a corridor between two states of being. Outside, the Andean Eastern Mountain Range or Cordillera Real appears, not seen so much as revealed: silent stone titans watching the pale tremble of the city below.

La Paz—reclining like something injured, something vast, caught between convulsion and sleep.

Illimani is more than a mountain. Illimani, sometimes blue, sometimes violet, is a sentinel from before the beginning of time. At sunset, its triple crown of ice glows, bloodied with saffron and ash. It looks like a petrified condor, wings high in a forgotten gesture of flight, forever grounded, forever hovering.

To the north, Mururata—flat-headed, sullen.

Then Chacaltaya, once the highest ski slope in the world. Snow is just a memory now; its white mantle melted by human greed.

Further north, Huayna Potosí, slender

and brooding.

These are presences—elders, spectres, lungs of the earth. Fifty million years old, maybe older. The people pray to them. Feed them. Fear them. Love them. As they love their own dead.

Their stories are woven like ponchos, thread by thread, time knotting itself into new forms. The longer the silence between myth and mouth, the more vivid the tale. This is how we first heard the story of Mururata. We were children then.

Mururata was once the greatest. He had desired Illimani, wanted her for himself. But Illimani already had a lover—Huayna Potosí, smaller, quick, brutal. It was he who struck Mururata with a slingshot. His head flew, arced across the Altiplano, and became Sajama, the highest of them all.

The mountains are Achachilas. Ancestors. Not gods, no—they are too human for that. They weep, thirst, sleep. They have tempers. They remember.

At the edge of El Alto, La Paz opens before you like a laceration—red, ragged, immense. It spreads downwards, as if collapsing into itself. Valleys claw through it. Hills rise with shacks like scabs. What once took hours to cross in taxis now slides beneath the gondolas of the cable cars— floating above alleys, ravines, roofs, like ghosts skimming the skin of the city. I watch the coloured lines sway in the wind and think: a loom. A weaving. A pulse.

*

I must have been five or six when we asked our parents about the people lying in the alley near Plaza Alonso de Mendoza, just beyond our street.

Their bodies curled in silence, resting against walls, sacks, each other. The way they lay—there was a shape to it. A kind of topography. It reminded me of the Cordillera, how it encircles the city in jagged embrace.

"They're surprised," Clara whispered in my ear. "They can see us looking."

"They are poor," my mother said. "People who suffer."

My father muttered something about alcohol. I could tell he was annoyed.

Once, Clara slipped away while mum was waiting by a corner shop. We ended up in the alley, holding the hand of a toothless woman seated in an alcove. Her smile was not human. It was deeper. A kind of crack in the world. She returned us gently to mother, as if she'd been watching over us. My mother cried, gave the woman a chocolate bar.

That night, we were lectured about danger. Clara nodded when they asked me if I understood.

Years passed, and the faces in the alleys reappeared—on hillsides, in caves by the Choqueyapu River, among eucalyptus and cold wind. The river that once split the colonists from the natives, now splitting time itself—one bank always watching the other.

Some of them had lived there for decades. Some only for a night. You didn't hear them. You saw only the trace, the absence shaped like a man. Clara would talk to them. She always talked. She was the one who moved toward people. I just listened.

If not for her, I might have never left

home.

She dragged me with her. Into corners. Into stories. Into silence. The people she met never spoke much of themselves. But they spoke of each other. Sometimes with words, sometimes without. Clara listened. Sometimes she answered aloud. Sometimes only in thought.

That is how we learned. Or dreamt we learned. Fragments. Names without faces. Faces without names. Stories stitched into the fabric of the city like veins under skin.

Sepia

They say Claudio Sanjinés was, in another incarnation or a fever dream mistaken for memory, a philosopher. A writer. A man of letters at the University's Faculty of Humanities. He taught literature, yes. Philosophy, yes. But also, the slow agony of language, the cold breath of metaphor, and the indecipherable hum that lives behind human speech. He was said to have known everything, and yet—he knew nothing of the abyss that would one day open beneath his feet.

They wonder, the people with dry tongues and logical minds, whether his fascination with Kierkegaard and the burning puzzles of existence might have prepared him for what came. But there are no preparations for that kind of rupture—when the soul is ripped from the inside out. There are experiences that rot every blueprint. They are black suns. No mind, no heart, no cathedral of the spirit can bear them.

Claudio had once lived in a golden frame: a brilliant wife, eyes like wet ash, and a daughter who laughed like wind running across paper. Until, one night, the world inverted itself. A taxi. A bend in the road. Rain, or divine contempt. A vehicle that became a sarcophagus, tumbling down a steep slope like a thought escaping from the skull. When the car ceased to be a car, it was only a twisted animal, silent and final. Inside: three corpses, one without a head.

It was said—no, murmured in the dark crevices of campus—that during a thunderous afternoon lecture on Kierkegaard, Claudio had begun to dissolve. Something in the Danish philosopher's cruel labyrinth of faith and pain had cracked open inside him. Abraham and his son. God and his knife. The lecture hall turned into a crypt. The audience into ghosts. Some said Claudio spoke in tongues. Others claimed he vanished in the middle of a sentence.

When Claudio returned home that night, the rain still clung to the walls. Policemen with wax faces and neighbours like mannequins broke the news with trembling hands. At the morgue, time became a flat, grey sound. And when he came back —if one could say he returned at all—he refused every word, every gesture. He clutched his ears, as if demons had taken residence there. "Stop screaming," he said, repeatedly. Even when no one spoke. "Please stop screaming."

He was not present at the funeral. His body lay sedated, abandoned to sleep in the ruined temple of his family's house. Weeks passed. People left food, messages, warmth. He received none of it. The curtains hung like dead birds. The doorbell was unstrung: an undesired violin. Cards and letters formed a nest of unopened grief at the threshold.

One day, the house breathed him out. He walked into the city's underworld and vanished.

He took nothing but a photograph and a tin box filled with sewing tools: needles, threads of colour, buttons and a small pair of retractable scissors that clicked like tiny jaws. From then on, he became the tailor of his own undoing.

*

His coat became a map—stitched from rags and leather scraps, each patch a continent of memory. Time stitched him too. His beard grew like ivy; his hair matted like forgotten wool. Dust made its home in him. The cave he chose as his dwelling was not just a hollow in the mountain—it was a threshold. Like Feliciano Sirpa, of whom Jaime Saenz once wrote, Claudio too crossed into the other side. Not death, exactly. Not life, either. Something in between.

He ceased to resemble a man. He became a hue: sepia, rust, ash. A walking photograph faded by rain and longing. He blended into his environment until no one could tell where Claudio ended, and where the rocks began.

They say sometimes we become the places we inhabit. But Claudio's case is stranger still: he became the silence between the places. The breath the city forgot to take.

He survived on cast-off fruits and market remains, and when he wanted a hot meal, he hung a rope around his shoulders and became a mule. A ghost-of-burden. People handed him weight, and he accepted it without question. His silence was a language of its own. He carried things the way some carry grief: without complaint, without explanation.

The city believed he lived in many places: the folds of Pura Pura, the shadows of Laikakota, the forgotten arteries of Llojeta. He may have bathed in the rivers that remembered old gods. He may have walked all the way to Río Abajo, his feet made of dust and memory. Some claimed to see him. Few dared speak to him. Fewer were believed.

*

One afternoon, climbing a hill in the South, we glimpsed a twitch in the earth. At first, we thought it was the light shifting. Then we saw him—blurred into the mountain's texture, like the static of a broken screen. Movement without movement. Clara tried to call him. He answered with a single gesture—a dismissal or a blessing—we couldn't tell.

He had absorbed the tone of the land: ochres, browns, the dry rust of twilight. The experience felt like watching the city's memory fade in real time. He looked like history unspooling in reverse. His carbon footprint was sub-zero. His presence: spectral and vast.

He gathered bones of the urban detritus: plastic and metal, cloth and stone. He made from them a palace of silence. A museum of resilience. In the cave, he was not alone—he lived with the spirits of thought, the phantoms of unfinished books, the echo of lectures that never ended. His mind, perhaps, became a theatre. His memories, scenes in a flickering film never made.

*

When we saw Feliciano Sirpa's coat—Jaime Saenz had once traded a new coat for it—we thought of Claudio. The coat was a relic, thick with history, its seams dense with madness and time. A stitched palimpsest. Each layer a whisper.

Inside its pockets, we imagined Claudio's picture—his wife and daughter, paused forever in some unreachable summer.

That moment called back the few, fleeting glimpses we had of Claudio. Was his wandering not a kind of philosophy? Was he not practising a deeper, more devout form of living thought?

Instead of writing about existence, he inhabited it—threaded his days into the void, stitched the world anew with every step.

And so, in the end, Claudio Sanjinés did not disappear. He became the needle. The thread. The cloak. The coat. He wore the city, and the city wore him.

They say that in time, the mountains forgot his name, but remembered his weight. The caves shifted slightly, as if making space for him to lie down more comfortably. And when he slept, it was not sleep in the ordinary sense—but a falling sideways into other strata of existence, where his wife and daughter walked through fog, speaking in the language of stones.

Sometimes, children playing near the quebradas would swear they saw a figure inside the rocks—not behind, but within—the way a dried flower is kept in glass. Others said he was two men: one who scavenged markets by day, and another who howled in the hills at night, blindfolded and barefoot, dancing with spirits only he could see.

Of course, these are stories. They multiply in the absence of truth. But what is truth, in a city like La Paz, where the streets coil like intestines, and memory leaks from the walls?

Some nights, in the Zona Sur, when fog descends like a shroud and dogs stop barking without reason, one might see a thin line of smoke rising from a hill.

The scent—not just of wood, but of burnt books and dried petals—drifts into the houses of the living. Some say it's Claudio, burning pages of a book he never wrote. Others claim he's summoning the past with bits of string, a tin of ash, and a pair of scissors once held by love.

*

One man, an old librarian who had shared lunch with Claudio once in the university's courtyard, claimed to have followed him, years later, from a distance. Said he watched him rummage through the remains of a broken television, pull out the circuitry, and place it reverently in his pocket.

"He's building something," the librarian said, "not just shelter—something else. A machine of memory, or maybe a device to communicate with the beyond."

He died shortly after, and no one

21

believed him.

*

We once met a woman who said she had seen Claudio during the winter of '83. She was selling oranges near the cemetery when he appeared, his face shadowed by a deformed hat stitched from pieces of burlap and leather. He approached her stall, not to buy—but to stare. She said he stared at the oranges as if he'd never seen colour before. Then he pulled from his coat a single copper button and placed it gently on the table, as if offering a gift to the sun.

She tried to speak, but he was already turning, already returning to the earth.

*

Over the years, some of us would catch glimpses. Not of Claudio himself, but

22

of his traces: a path of perfectly aligned bottle caps stretching along a ravine; a crude wooden frame hung on a tree, framing nothing but fog; a coat stitched to a cactus, its sleeves flapping in the wind like spectral wings.

These were not random acts. They were messages. Notes from the underworld. Glyphs from a philosopher who had shed language.

And though he never returned to the University, his presence began to haunt it. Students reported hearing footsteps in empty corridors. Books on existentialism moved of their own accord. In lecture halls, the temperature dropped when his name was mentioned. In one classroom, a cracked photograph of Kierkegaard began to weep a thin, oily resin.

Some dismissed these accounts as hysteria. But those who had known Claudio—the real Claudio—said nothing. They only looked away.

*

Years later, a group of archaeology students exploring the outer edges of Laikakota claimed to find a cave unlike any they had seen before. Inside, walls were etched with what appeared to be diagrams: maps of a world turned inside-out.

They also found piles of fabric. Bones of furniture made from rusted bedframes. A cup fashioned from an animal skull. A book, or something like a book, made of stitched, together leaves and animal skin. They left the cave in silence and never returned.

When we walked the hills again in the

early 2000s, we no longer searched for Claudio. We searched for echoes. We thought we might find his coat, or a whisper, or a thread. Instead, we found a hole in the ground.

Inside, perfectly arranged: three stones, a pair of scissors, and a fragment of mirror. When Clara looked into it, she did not see her face—only the flicker of fire, and two shadows holding hands in a place beyond mourning.

And yet, even that vision in the mirror—two shadows holding hands, flickering like the last coherence of a dream—was only the beginning of another descent. For the hills were changing; the city was exhaling in long, tired breaths, and the air carried something brittle, like the cracked glaze of forgotten pottery.

In the following days, Clara could not sleep. She said the mirror fragment had left a tingle in her palm, as though it clung to her with a faint, secret heartbeat. At night, she dreamt she was walking through the caves beneath the city—caves no map acknowledged—each more narrow than the last. Something followed her: a rhythm, a clicking, like metal jaws opening and closing in the dark. When she woke, the sound continued for a moment before vanishing into daylight. I thought it was memory misfiring in the skull. But she insisted: "No. It's sewing something. Someone is stitching me."

I laughed, though I shouldn't have.

Because soon I heard it too.

The clicking came first at dusk: faint, tentative, as if tracing the edges of our thoughts. Then it moved closer. The city itself seemed to respond—lamps flickered; dogs paused mid-bark; the walls leaned slightly inward, as though listening. A thread, invisible but taut, stretched from some unknown burrow in the mountains to the fragile chambers of our own nights.

Word began to drift through the markets: a man of rags had been seen near Pampahasi, standing perfectly still in the rain. Another sighting near Villa Fátima—just a coat draped over what might have been a human form, or might have been a pole. In San Pedro, a child said she'd seen a figure at dawn bending over a puddle, cutting its reflection into strips with a pair of silver jaws.

But these were only weather reports from the other side. Shadows of shadows.

We returned to the hill where we had found the mirror. The hole was deeper now.

As if someone—or something—had been digging from below. Three stones remained, but the scissors were gone. And the mirror fragment lay shattered into seven pieces, each one reflecting a different sky.

Clara knelt. She touched one shard. Her breath caught. She said the reflection showed not her face, not the sky—nothing she could name. Only movement. Only a slow, spiraling descent, like a soul remembering its fall.

We covered the hole with earth and stones, though we knew it made no difference. You cannot bury what was never meant to stay above ground.

After that day, the city behaved strangely. Walls sweated at noon. The pavements cracked in shapes resembling letters—letters we could not read, though some resembled diagrams from the cave. The fog came earlier, thicker, and lingered like a shawl forgotten over the city. And the people… the people walked more softly, as if not to disturb something sleeping beneath the surface.

Rumors swelled.

A woman from Sopocachi found a trail of buttons leading from her doorstep to a vacant lot, aligned in a perfect spiral. In Llojeta, two teenagers stumbled on a humanoid silhouette carved into stone, stitched around the edges with what looked like copper wire.

None of this was news. Not really. Only confirmations of what we already knew but refused to articulate: Claudio had continued to unmake himself. Or remake himself. Or slip sideways into some geometry of the city invisible to common eyes.

One evening, as fog descended and the city dissolved into a penumbra of murmurs, we found ourselves walking without plan, without thought, guided by a faint metallic click that seemed to rise and fall with our steps. It led us past the cemetery—always the cemetery, with its elegant boredom—and toward the silent flank of the hills.

There, the earth seemed thinner. As if the membrane between this world and the other had worn down to a breath.

We heard a soft cadence: snip, snip, snip. Then the unmistakable rasp of thread being pulled taut.

We did not see him. Not fully. But for a moment, a silhouette formed between two rocks: a coat made of mismatched fabrics, billowing as though it were breathing; a pair of hands working with impossible calm; something glimmering at the fingertips—metal, maybe bone. And behind him, the faint shape of a doorway in the stone, lit from inside by a pale, lunar glow.

Clara whispered: "He's mending something."

The silhouette turned—slowly, like an old photograph dragged across time. Not to face us, exactly, but to acknowledge us. A nod that could have been gratitude, warning, or farewell.

Then the doorway folded shut. The rocks reassembled. The hill became a hill again.

We stood for a long time, unsure if we

had witnessed a visitation or a memory replaying itself in the dark matter of the city.

On the way back, Clara thought she understood at last. Claudio had not gone mad. He had not fled grief. He had not fractured under the black sun that had swallowed his world.

No.

He was repairing it.

Somewhere beneath the skin of La Paz, in the veins of its earth, in the lungs of its stone, he was stitching existence—the torn fabric of what had been, what might have been, and what still longed to be.

And perhaps, one day, when the city inhales just right and the mountains tilt their faces toward eternity, we will feel a small, almost imperceptible tightening in the air.

A thread pulled through.

A seam closed.

A world mended ever so slightly by the hands of a man who once taught literature, philosophy, and the slow, tender agony of language.

A man who became a needle.

A needle who became a city.

And a city that—on certain nights—still remembers his weight.

Purple

Some people exist so deeply within the folds of La Paz that they become part of the city's stitching. Others, however, are too vivid to disappear. They remain visible not because they are real, but because reality itself is too dazed to swallow them.

The Purple Man belonged to neither category.

Clara once said he glowed. We were making a collage—an old ritual we invented to confuse time—when she held up an image of a blue-haired woman in a yellow coat. She placed her on a grainy black-and-white photograph of an urban scene and said, "Look, she glows... just like him."

The Purple Man.

More apparition than citizen.

More static than statue.

He stood in the city centre—always still, always silent, a magenta bruise on the grey face of La Paz.

His skin shimmered in hues that hinted at both a chemical and natural world. His hands were like wet flowers, his face and bald head sunlit from beneath the flesh. He wore a suit once grey, now consumed by violet—the kind of suit worn by the forgotten, the resigned, or the initiated. His shirt's light collar was also tinted in purple tones.

His silence was so absolute, it made noise.

*

They say he bathed in the violet discharge of a textile factory that bled its colours into the Choqueyapu. That he lived near the river's muttering stones. That he was dipped, daily, in some kind of industrial baptism, until the pigment entered his bones.

We saw him there once, moving across the riverbed like a heavy hum. It hadn't rained in days. The river was a sleeping vein. He knelt beside a fluorescent puddle—radioactive, comic-book glow—and dabbed at his face with cupped hands.

Clara asked, "What if he's not dyeing himself? What if he's leaking colour from within?"

*

People did not know what to do with him. A man in a suit that defied every category. He was neither beggar nor performer, neither lunatic nor worker. He stood too still to be alive, too alive to be ignored. He was the absence of category. And yet, a child might laugh, a dog might bark, and he would remain—motionless, embedded.

Only when he walked—when the spell wore off—did he seem real again. But only barely.

He was not invisible. No. He was what happens when visibility overflows and becomes unbearable.

*

One day on Yanacocha Street, Clara leaned in to sniff him. She wanted to know if he smelled like lavender. I watched her nose hover close to his shoulder. She found nothing—no scent—only a loose thread, thin as a vein, dancing in her breath. She plucked it gently and walked away, clutching it like a relic.

We examined it together—its curl, its flicker. I imagined it weaving itself around our fingers, like stripy grey and pink worms knitting gloves of silence. When we looked up, he had vanished. The thread pulsated in our palms like a heartbeat.

That night, I dreamt of the hills of Aranjuez—painted in impossible shades of ochre and amethyst. I buried my hands in the clay and felt it exhale, as if the earth were dreaming me back.

*

The Purple Man did not haunt the museums or cathedrals. He hovered just outside them. In places where time cracked open and let light leak in. One twilight, near

Jaén Street, we saw a woman dressed in black—floating, barely touching the cobblestones. Clara followed her until she vanished into a wall that had no door.

Moments later, a procession emerged from around the corner: drums, flutes, smoke, confetti. Six men carried a giant stone toad wrapped in streamers, its mouth puffing cigarette smoke. People danced in fevered circles. Libations were spilled. Words were addressed to stone. All around: the sense of a city remembering something too old to name.

We asked no questions. We had learned not to.

*

The Purple Man reappeared often in Zona Norte. His presence reshaped our plans. We would drop whatever task was at hand

and follow him at a respectful distance, like mourners chasing a forgotten saint. We believed, in those moments, that we were not in the present. That the air was different. Time slowed to a syrupy crawl.

Once, he stood at the edge of Riosinho Square, facing North. He was entirely still—but we felt his eyes reaching out beyond the horizon. Even without motion, his body vibrated with a kind of knowing. He was not watching the city—he was remembering it before it happened.

When he walked, we followed. He passed the Bus Terminal, turned down Beni Street, then disappeared into a side alley like a dissolving echo.

At the intersection, there was no one. Only light.

Not the sun, but something else. A magenta glaze had poured over the sky, the walls, the windows. The cobblestones shimmered as if polished from the inside out. Even our shadows had turned violet. We inhaled. The light entered our lungs.

That night, I dreamt again.

But this time, the Purple Man spoke.

Not with words—his mouth remained closed. But his jacket opened like a curtain, and inside was a stairwell. We descended. The walls were stitched fabric. The air was thick with indigo dust. On the final step, we saw a pile of thread, neatly arranged in the shape of a human heart.

Clara reached for it.

It throbbed.

The rhythm was faint, yet unmistakable—like the heartbeat of something that should not have been alive, yet refused to die. Clara held her breath. The threads—violet, plum, bruised-lilac—shivered in her hand as though stirred by a wind we could not feel. The stairwell walls, stitched from mismatched fabrics, tightened around us. A soft creaking echoed from somewhere above, or below, or inside the fabric itself.

Then the heart exhaled.

A cloud of purple dust rose, drifting into our faces. It carried a smell like wet metal and forgotten violets. My lungs tightened. Time thickened into molasses. Clara staggered back—but did not let go. Of course she didn't. She never let go of anything that pulsed.

The heart unfurled.

Not violently, not suddenly. It loosened like a fist opening after decades of holding something immeasurable. The threads unknit themselves, revealing not organs but shapes—geometries that quivered like light trapped in cloth. There was a square that refused to have corners, a circle that pounded as if breathing, and a line that bent toward us like a beckoning finger.

We thought, "It wants to be followed."

But the shape did not move. Instead, the stairwell itself did.

A tremor ran through the space. The steps extended downward, growing, multiplying, descending into an ever-deepening night. The fabric walls stretched, pulling new seams into existence with an audible stitch-stitch-stitch, like the Purple Man's hands were still working somewhere in the dark.

We stepped down.

The stairs led us into a chamber made of shadow and lacquered air. At its centre stood a loom—massive, ancient, trembling. Its beams were carved from petrified light. Its threads were strands of night itself, pulled taut between forces unseen. And sitting before it, unmoving, was a figure.

The Purple Man.

Or the outline of him. His suit glowed faintly, as if absorbing and leaking colour simultaneously. His bald head shone with a subdermal radiance, a lantern buried under flesh. His hands, resting on his knees, dripped slow droplets of violet—like sap from a wounded tree.

He did not look at us. Not directly. Yet something in him noticed us, like a memory twitching awake. The air grew dense. My knees weakened.

Clara whispered, "He's weaving."

But his hands were still.

We looked again—and realised the loom was moving on its own. Threads of shadow and light intertwined, forming images that flickered in and out of coherence: streets, faces, doorways that opened into rivers, rivers that opened into sky. Then we saw ourselves—tiny silhouettes walking through a violet haze.

Clara gasped. The threads rearranged. Now we saw the city—La Paz—its hills trembling like lungs. The towers bowed. The houses leaned. The streets coiled into serpentine ribbons that pulsed with pigment.

The Purple Man finally raised his head.

His eyes were not eyes. They were windows into some inner phosphorescence, a liquefied violet shimmering with impossible depth. He opened his mouth—not to speak but to exhale something that was not quite breath. A vapour. A colour. A sound.

We heard it in our bones.

A hum—not human, not mechanical—something like the resonance of a mountain remembering its origin. The loom responded, speeding up. Its threads crackled. The images shifted violently.

We saw the river. The Choqueyapu.

But not as it is now. As it was before the city. As it was when it first dreamed of water. Then the dream cracked. Colours poured out. Violet, magenta, purple—an entire spectrum bleeding like a wound.

"You see, he wasn't dyed," Clara murmured. "He's the leak."

And it was true.

The Purple Man's skin was not stained. It was illuminated from an inner rupture—an overflow of the city's oldest memory, a pigment of origin, something primordial and unnamed.

He stood.

The chamber trembled. The loom halted mid-image. Darkness swam around us, thick with tension.

He extended a hand toward Clara.

Not touching. Just offering.

The threads of the unknit heart pulsed in her palm.

Then something impossible happened.

The threads rose—levitated—writhing like living veins. They slithered upward, weaving themselves into the Purple Man's outstretched hand. One by one, they burrowed into his palm, disappearing beneath the skin with soft, wet sounds.

The glow intensified.

His veins lit up—a map of luminescent channels. His chest shone through the fabric of his suit. His skull flickered like a lantern caught between worlds.

Then he lowered his hand.

And with a faint bow—reverent, exhausted, eternal—he turned and walked into the wall of shadow behind him. The wall rippled, absorbed him, closed.

We were alone.

The loom unravelled. The chamber dimmed. The stairwell contracted, its fabric walls quivering like tired lungs. A wind rose from below—cold, patient, ancient.

We climbed back up.

At the top, we found ourselves not in the dream, not in the room, but in the middle of Mercado Camacho at dusk. People moved around us normally. Cars passed. The smell of fried anticuchos drifted lazily.

No one had noticed our return.

But the sky above—once ordinary—now shimmered with a faint violet bruise.

Clara looked at her hand.

The threads were gone.

But her palm glowed faintly, as if inked by something that was not colour but memory.

"We weren't following him," she said. "He was stitching us into the city."

And as we walked home, I realised she was right.

La Paz had shifted.

And we had become part of the new seam.

White

We floated above Alasitas as though the cable car had snapped from time, and the air in the cabin was holy and thick with the gasp of the dead. Incense spiralled into our lungs like phantom smoke, and as we peered down on the stalls—those obsessive arrangements of desire shrunk to fingernail size—my eyes swam in a white fog of remembrance. As it happened every year in late January, the fair was there. Always calling us. Always waiting for us. A recurring dream hidden behind a hill.

Clara said nothing. Her reflection was pale that day, almost translucent. Maybe the whiteness had entered her, too.

Below us: the silent hysteria of tiny things.

Toilet paper, bottles of beer and whisky, university diplomas, miniature pickup trucks with real suspension. A single-bite-sized fried quail egg sandwich. You could eat your future here. You could taste it, chew it, lose a tooth in it.

We passed a stall that sold mini divorce papers, folded neatly inside microscopic folders. "Look," Clara said, holding one up to her eye. "It's already signed, someone will be free soon…"

You could wish for anything. But the wish had to be believable. Belief was the currency.

A street drunk buying a stack of mini-US dollars would likely get nothing but another day. But a wheelbarrow? A sewing machine? Those were closer to God. Ironically, the fake money was cheaper than the tiny shovels. Maybe because the shovels were forged by real hands. Paper can lie. Metal sings.

That day, we bought bricks, tiles, cement, and tools the size of mouse bones. We walked slowly to the corner where a man in a poncho waved burning rosemary in the air, painting invisible words into the ether. We bowed to the smoke. It knew more than we did.

*

But my thoughts returned to another man—one who had no stall, no licence, no saints or signs. Just a can.

A rusty can, stabbed with holes to breathe fire.

He called us caseros and always asked for payment in drink, though he accepted money when pressed. His clothes were stiff with soot and spilt wishes. His hands were swollen, red, the same hue as his round, sweating face.

The smell of rosemary and alcohol swirled from him like weather.

He blessed our miniatures by wrapping them in last year's newspaper—last year's news, last year's crimes—and waving them over the smoke while murmuring something between a prayer and a joke.

He sang in Aymara, Pukina, or something older. We could never remember the melody, but the shape of it stuck in our ribs.

*

His body reeked of death, but kindly. As if death could bless things too.

That was the year when Manuel Pereira reappeared. He had been missing for years, and then, suddenly, he seemed to be in every rumour.

First, a cousin in the elevator muttered his name. Then someone at the market swore he'd seen him, barefoot, selling broken phones near the bus terminal.

We had known him before. Or thought we had.

Manuel, who danced to Nancy Sinatra in hot pants and leather boots.

Manuel, who taught us about the body's duplicity. Who played director and diva, and child all at once. Who filmed his parents' silences.

Who wore lipstick before he had pubic hair. Who said, "We are lesbians trapped in men's bodies," and meant it.

He had floated in his own Alasitas—a pocket—sized world sculpted from VHS tapes and dreams. His parents gave him everything, and so he believed in everything.

He once climbed onto the window ledge of our eighth-floor apartment and dangled his legs into the void. When a girl playing on the ground floor rejected him, he stared down into the courtyard abyss and inhaled the sky.

He didn't jump. But something fell. Maybe belief. Maybe his reflection.

Clara's eyes glowed after that. I almost saw it. Something ignited in her. They became inseparable—sucked into each other like two white pills fizzing in the same glass.

Then came the rituals of collapse:

joints passed between trembling fingers, cocaine cut with ID cards and snorted through rolled banknotes, or scooped with tiny spoons, kisses shaped like knives.

Parties blurred into weeks. Time shrank, then multiplied. Clara gasped in numbers. Manuel stopped blinking.

They smoked everything. They drank everything. They reversed the logic of mornings.

*

I watched, like a fly stapled to the wall, my wings folded in shame.

Manuel vanished again. This time for real.

We heard stories. That he prostituted himself near San Francisco Square.

That he'd been caught selling drugs or shoplifting mirrors.

That he had HIV and bled on purpose to keep others away.

That he kept a blade in his mouth. That he never slept. He only spoke in facial expressions now. That his parents had disowned him—not for the drugs, not for the theft, but because he had failed to be them.

The last time anyone saw him, he was chained to a pipe in a hospital basement. He had become so light, they said, the nurses barely noticed him. His skin turned white. Translucent. Like paper.

He had become a miniature. A tiny, breakable thing. A relic.

*

The final blessing never came.

Clara walked to the edge of the river and tossed a handful of crushed rosemary into the Choqueyapu. The wind ignored her. The smoke refused to rise.

I still dream of him.

He stands on a bridge in white boots, covered in ash.

He holds a hairbrush like a microphone. His voice is thin, like a thread.

Behind him: a million toy houses burning in silence.

He mouths the words, "These boots are made for walking…" but no sound comes out.

Then he turns, stares straight into me, and lifts one tiny, blistered hand.

I always wake up before he waves.

And the waking is worse than the dream. Because the dream has its own rules—absurd, merciful rules—but the daylight carries his absence like a bruise beneath the skin.

I walk through the morning as if I'd been dropped from a great height into a city made entirely of afterimages.

The cobblestones glint with a thin frost that has no right to exist in the heat of late January, and I know it's him. Manuel. Hiding in the cracks of the pavement, or maybe in the fogged breath of the first microbusero warming his hands over a glass of api.

Winter has invaded our bones early this year. Clara stares straight ahead as if the city were a long corridor she is determined to reach the end of. The wind of La Paz is a creature—capricious, vengeful—and that morning it braided itself through her hair as though searching for the parts of her she has forgotten to protect.

"We should go back to the fair," she murmurs suddenly. "Maybe he's waiting there."

But Alasitas is a one-way dream. Once it dissolves into February, it becomes memory—stale incense, expired wishes. You can't go back. Not unless you slip through a crack in the day.

Still, we walk toward the city centre as if the fair might bloom again under our steps. And in the traffic-clogged streets, with the hills retaining their solemn gaze, I swear the smell of rosemary finds us—thin, burned, insistent. It trails us like a ghost seeking purchase.

Clara stops.

"There," she says, pointing to a corner where a man with a wheeled cart sells old cassette tapes, each sun-bleached and warped by heat. The titles run together like melted chocolate. Among them: Nancy Sinatra's Greatest Hits, its plastic case cracked down the spine.

A shiver moves through us both.

Clara buys it without bargaining. The vendor watches her with an expression that feels too knowing, as though he's seen the ghost in her pupils. He asks if she wants a Walkman too, but she shakes her head. "No need," she says. "I can already hear it."

And she's right. Something in the air

begins to pulse—faint, rhythmic. A drum heartbeat stitched with a whisper of melody. Not quite the song, but the ghost of it. The city absorbs it. The power lines tremble. Even the pigeons seem to tilt their heads toward the sound.

We follow it down Calle Potosí.

The rhythm leads us into a narrow alley—a place melting together shadows and forgotten trash. There, leaning against a wall plastered with election posters and theatre flyers, stands a figure.

At first we think it's him. But the figure is too tall. Too clean. Too anchored to the ground.

And then the figure opens its mouth.

A voice spills out—thin, quivering, as if the throat producing it is not entirely present. The words melt into the hum of the city.

"Listen."

The voice—if it can be called a voice—forms something like a sentence:

"Te está esperando…"

He is waiting for you.

But the mouth does not move.

The sound seems to come from somewhere behind the figure, or beneath it, or through it. The alley vibrates with an invisible tremor, a ripple in the air. The posters flutter though there is no wind. A pipe drips water that steams upon touching the ground.

Then the figure blinks—and vanishes.

Not dramatically. Not mystically. Simply: gone. As if it had been painted on a piece of glass someone quietly slid away.

Clara steps forward, trembling. What she finds on the wall is a smear—a faint streak of ash. Shaped like a thumbprint. Or a burnt kiss.

She presses her hand to it.

Her entire body stiffens.

I hear something—something I should not hear:

Footsteps. Bare. Approaching. From behind us. From above us. From beneath us.

The alley shudders.

And then—

A flash of white boots turning a

corner.

We chase them, breathless, stumbling, our shadows scrambling ahead of us like frightened animals. The boots vanish into a passageway between two buildings, a tight concrete throat that seems to swallow light whole. We follow, deeper, until the world narrows to a single point of violet dusk.

There, in the half-dark, we find a plastic bag caught on a nail. Inside: a comb. Cheap. Slightly cracked. The kind Manuel always carried, flicking it open like a magician conjuring a final trick.

Clara lifts it. A strand of hair clings to the teeth—impossibly thin, almost translucent. When she holds it up, light filters through it like milk through gauze.

"It's… white," she whispers.

White like paper.

White like the hospital basement.

White like belief falling from a window ledge.

She pockets the comb with the delicacy of a priest collecting relics.

*

Back in the sunlit street, life continues, indifferent.

But Clara's eyes—they glow again. Not with joy, but with an old, familiar ignition. The same surreal flame that lit her years ago at the edge of collapse. A dangerous radiance. A brilliance sharpened by grief.

"Tonight," she says, "we go to the river."

The river's stones mutter in languages only the dead understand, I already know we will find something there—big or small, real or imaginary, alive or tiny enough to fit in a pocket.

A sign.

A thread.

A miniature of him.

Because Manuel has returned—not in flesh, not in thought, but in the only form this city ever grants its lost children:

Echo.

Ash.

And the faint, unbearable hum of a song the world tries to forget, but cannot silence.

Not yet.

Red

The night in La Paz isn't black—it's red. A thick, bleeding red. The kind that drips from the edges of time itself.

The kind that trickles from the mouth of a cracked bottle of pisco.

There are places where the walls drink too, where shadows lurch softly and the stray dogs walk backwards. Places where reality tilts—just a little—and you can hear the dead's thoughts behind people's eyes.

Leonardo Trigo, or Trago, as everyone called him, lived in such places. He didn't rent a room; he rented silence from the alleyways.

He was round like a drum, with skin that glistened like wet plaster, and his breath came in short puffs, like someone forever ascending stairs that no longer exist.

He wore whatever he found. One day, a shawl and a long skirt. Another day, an old woolly jumper on top of a pair of baggy trousers made from canvas.

He spoke to his empty paint cans, like they were disappointing children or perhaps stubborn spirits. No one dared correct him. It wasn't clear he was wrong.

He drank—not out of thirst, but as a form of remembrance. Alcohol Caiman or Caña Fuerte, sometimes cut with sweet red powder that turned the stomach but calmed the soul. It burned going down. Burned like memory. Burned like truth.

He said he once studied at San Andrés University. Maybe he did. He also said the President once kissed his forehead and called him "el futuro."

He said he had a daughter made entirely of charcoal. That she lived in a closet and sang arias to the rats. He said many things. The point was never to believe him—the point was to listen.

Clara met him first in a cavern bar near the barrio of San Pedro, where the tables were always sticky and the light dim. He was painting the wall behind the urinals, a mural of a condor with seven eyes and no wings, each eye reflecting a different ruin of the city.

Clara said it was the first time she had seen a man paint directly onto the bare walls of a building. She laughed and fell in love with the idea of him. Not him—never him—but the idea. That he was proof you could live inside madness and still speak truth and poetry. And that he made her laugh!

Apart from painting on walls, he also wrote poems that bled through them. He recited such poems under bridges.

He was brilliant. He was unbearable. He was a genius, which in this city is a kind of curse.

He once painted the angels he saw crawling in the gutters, and demons selling snacks on the steps of San Francisco Cathedral.

He spoke to invisible friends. Not hallucinations—companions. He claimed to be translating their language into poetry, colour, and form. It all sounded like laughter breaking through chipped teeth.

*

Red isn't just the alcohol or the paint. It's also the blood. Because Leonardo began to cough. First in winter, then with the dawn.

He said the city had begun to repaint him from the inside. His lungs now made of dust, his ribs hollowed brushes. Each wheeze was a brush stroke.

He moved from place to place like a shadow, looking for the right wall.

The abandoned bus near Cementerio General.

The rooftop above Avenida Buenos Aires.

A broken fountain where the water hadn't run in a decade, but he swore it called his name every night, at midnight.

He painted until the colours ran away from him. Murals of women without eyes, cathedrals melting like wax, skeletons reading newspapers. Murals that appeared and disappeared in a day, like hallucinations you could touch.

Once, he painted a stairwell so perfectly that no one realised it didn't lead anywhere. A woman climbed it and walked into the air. She didn't scream, just dissolved mid-step like she'd remembered something too late.

*

When he died—if that's what happened—they found him curled beneath his final wall:

A man with no face, painting with smoke.

A Virgin with rust for tears.

The city trapped inside a jar.

The municipality arrived.

Bureaucracy is bleach.

They painted over everything.

Left no plaque. No photograph. No silence. Just white.

But the alley behind San Pedro never truly emptied. The air is still thick there. Heavy like a blanket soaked in wine and salt. Some nights, children hear a brush scraping the bricks. The red returns, faintly, as if trying to remember itself.

They say Leonardo Trago still paints.

With blood, with fog, with shadow.

They say the Virgin bleeds once more.

And if you pass by, late enough,

drunk enough, ruined enough—

You might just see a face staring at you from a wall that wasn't there yesterday.

And it might look like yours.

Because nothing dies in this city.

Not really.

It just gets painted over.

What no one ever told you—and what Leonardo insisted was the only truth worth knowing—is that the red of La Paz is not a colour but a hunger. A slow, patient appetite that seeps from the stones and the night-breath of the city, creeping into the lungs of those who walk its slopes after midnight. You don't see it at first. It hides in the corners of old photographs and in the folds of dirty curtains. But one day it finds you. And once it has you, it never lets go.

Leonardo used to say the red had found him the year he slept inside a dismantled kiosk on Calle Linares, curled around a bucket of half-finished paint like a man embracing a dying dog. "It taught me how to see," he whispered once, to no one in particular, as if the city itself had enrolled him in its private academy. "The city speaks in red. You just have to bleed a little to understand it."

People avoided him, yes—but gently, like you would avoid a sleeping saint whose dreams might be dangerous to interrupt. Mothers steered their children away from him while still making the sign of the cross, unsure whether to fear him or pray for him. Taxi drivers swore they saw him glowing faintly in their rearview mirrors, even when he wasn't there. Drunks followed him, convinced he knew where the night really began.

Clara said Leonardo walked like a candle melting from the inside out, slow and deliberate, leaving a trail of something warm behind. She liked that about him—his strange softness, the way he apologised to walls before painting on them. He treated buildings like people, and people like passing shadows.

He once told her that every wall has a pulse, faint but real. "Some walls are ready to confess," he murmured, his tongue stained red from drink. "Others prefer to lie. But each one wants something painted on it. They just don't always know what."

Leonardo listened. That was his real gift. He listened to stones and pipes and water tanks. He pressed his ear to the pavement and nodded as though receiving instructions. The city was his teacher, his tormentor, his accomplice.

But the coughing got worse.

Some said he'd inhaled too much solvent; others said it was the cold; others swore that the Virgin of the Cracked Pavement had cursed him for painting her barefoot and laughing. But Leonardo waved away every explanation with a trembling hand. "I'm being repainted," he insisted. "Colour by colour. Layer by layer."

He claimed he could feel the walls inside him shifting, brick grinding against brick. "The city wants me to become it," he said once, with the serene terror of a man who is both proud and doomed. "Eventually, I'll be nothing but a mural waiting to happen."

He wasn't wrong.

The night he disappeared from the rooftop above Avenida Buenos Aires, the sky had turned a colour no one could name—something like red, but mixed with a thickness that made the air feel edible. Witnesses say they saw him climbing a ladder that wasn't really there, ascending toward a piece of wall that had peeled itself open like a raw wound. They said he stepped inside the wall. Not through it—inside it.

By dawn the mural he'd painted was gone.

But the wall was warm to the touch.

And on its surface, beneath the plaster, you could feel the faintest heartbeat.

His final work—the one beneath which he curled to die, or vanish, or transform—was painted with a precision unnerving even to his admirers. A man with no face painting with smoke; a Virgin shedding rust like centuries of sorrow; a jar containing the city, shaking slightly, as if something inside it wanted out.

The municipal workers arrived with buckets of white paint and the calm cruelty of men who believe they are fixing something. They joked among themselves, smoking cigarettes and humming cumbia, unaware that each stroke of their brushes erased something living. They covered the Virgin first. Then the faceless man. And finally the jar.

By the time they were done, the alley was spotless.

Which is to say, lifeless.

But La Paz does not accept erasure so

easily. The city is older than bureaucracy, older than ceremonies, older than its own streets. So the red began to seep back through the white paint like blood through a badly wrapped bandage.

Quiet at first. Then bolder.

Some nights, the wall sweats.

Some nights, it cries rust.

Children swear they've heard murmurs—wet, shaky, like someone rinsing their lungs and squeezing them dry. Old women crossing the alley whisper prayers without looking up. Dogs refuse to pass through. And drunkards—Leonardo's true congregation—report seeing shapes moving on the mural-less wall, as if the painting is trying to remember itself.

One swore he saw a face appear—his

own, but stretched and hollow, as though the wall had decided to imitate him out of boredom.

Another saw Leonardo's shawl fluttering in a wind that didn't exist.

Years later, Clara claimed she sometimes felt fingers brushing her wrist as she walked through that alley. Not grabbing. Not threatening. Just checking if she was still there.

Leonardo was always like that—making sure no one vanished without being witnessed.

They say the red is thickest now behind San Pedro. That if you lean close enough, you can hear a brush tapping inside the plaster. A steady rhythm. Patient. Unfinished.

They say he is painting new walls now.

Invisible ones.

Between people.

Across their thoughts.

Onto their dreams.

And perhaps that's the truest curse of La Paz:

Nothing is ever gone or dead, just waiting for the next coat of paint.

Green

Those invisible by day sometimes become sighs and shadows at night.

At the crooked corner on a northeast hill where Indaburo meets Jaén Street stands the House of the Green Cross, a colonial stone monument to the memory of the city.

Here, the walls hum stories of the past, and voices ride the air like spectral panpipes. Those who live nearby speak of flickers, apparitions, and footsteps not their own. Shades that cling and groan.

Long ago, to hold back these restless echoes, or to mark the place for those who had inherited the role of the Spanish Inquisition, an iron cross was fixed to the wall beside a narrow veranda window.

Today, four green bulbs shine faintly, a subtle light, like veins of emerald flowing through the dark.

But the spectres laugh at such barriers—phantoms still brush shoulders with late wanderers, carelessly bumping into the living. Perhaps the spirits are drawn less by haunted history and more by the growing clatter of watering holes in the area.

Beneath this colonial beauty, once a cellar cradled a small bar—Bocaisapo— between 1997 and 2017.

Named for a flower shaped like a frog's open mouth, its heart was a toad, sculpted heavy and solemn, guarding the womb-like space that held bohemians, artists, and something older—telluric, spectral, a heartbeat from the earth.

*

One afternoon, don Cayo wandered along Calle Linares, high on the northwest slope. From a shadowed shop, a murmur rippled out—a soft plea, carried on the thin air. He paused, bent his head through the threshold, and asked softly:

"Yes?"

"Hi," croaked the voice, like a rattle from the stone toad perched by the door, guarding a mountain of old weavings.

"Little mama! What do you want?"

"Please get me out of here. I'm tired of watching this place. Help me, and I'll watch over you."

"But I have little money. I'm furnishing a tavern, small budget. Surely you cost more than I can pay..."

"Exactly. But I'm worth far less than I seem. Just ask."

After whispers traded like secrets, don Cayo agreed to try. He stepped inside and faced the owner, pointing:

"How much for the toad, señora?"

"Hahaha! Not for sale, señor. But I have smaller ones—frogs, snakes, lizards, fish—look." She rifled through dusty shelves.

"No, I want this one. Tell me your price."

"It guards the shop. Not for sale."

Don Cayo left, the toad's quiet promise trailing after him:

"Be persistent, I will help you."

*

Days blurred into weeks. Each passing by the shop, the toad's voice pulled him closer, until finally he returned with money and resolve.

"How are you, señora? I'm here for

the toad, with enough to pay and replace it. Please."

"I already told you, it guards the shop," she said, wary. "I never planned to sell."

"If the shop is yours, you can decide. Please let me buy it…"

"Many things have disappeared lately…"

"I will pay well, and I'll also bring a ritual mesa, for protection against thieves."

Negotiations stretched long into twilight. Finally, don Cayo won the toad's freedom, after organising special libations for its removal from the shop.

Together with the taxi driver, they carried the heavy stone guardian to the cab's back seat—blanket laid like an altar. Don Cayo sat beside it, both silent companions through the city's twists and turns.

At the House's cellar, the toad sighed as it touched the wooden bar. The taxi driver glanced around, seeing only shadows, took his fare, and accepted a cold drink.

"Thank you for bringing our friend home," said Don Cayo, the toad smiling in its quiet, ancient way.

*

Doña Teresa arrived later, heart warmed by the presence that had haunted don Cayo's words for weeks. They trimmed costs, built rough platforms and tables, simple, honest wood to welcome their tribe. Basic crockery, easy chairs, the bare bones of a home.

"Look at her. Smell her. Hear her old, deep voice," Don Cayo said to Teresa.

"She's wonderful," she smiled.

"It's settled." Don Cayo pulled an Astoria cigarette, lit it, and placed it in the toad's mouth slit. He opened a beer, poured two glasses, and spilt a splash over the stone.

"To our new best friend."

"To you, little mama," Teresa toasted, beer dripping like blessings.

Smoke curled white—good omen, they said.

Don Cayo laid coca leaves before the toad, then placed leaves behind his own lips, spines cut away—ancient ritual, communion with earth.

*

The bar thrived. The toad sat high, queen of the back room, gathering offerings of coca, cigarettes, and droplets of beer. Artists, poets, street children—no one turned away, no one cast out.

But seasons turned, and fortune waned. Sales dipped, debts mounted. One night, don Cayo confronted the toad:

"What's wrong? You promised success. I pay rent, staff, bills... I give you leaves, smoke, and drink. I dance for you. What more?"

The toad's voice was slow and weary:

"You feed me well. Your music warms me. But you are free. You walk the sun and moon. I am trapped, unseen sky, no stars. Is this fair?"

From this, the Guild of the Toad was born. Every year on Bocaisapo's anniversary, the stone idol is carried through the streets—Indaburo to Sanjines, to Ingavi, Pichincha, back home—torches and drums, a procession of reverence and wild joy, rain or shine. Though most often rain.

*

The first time we entered Bocaisapo, we discovered that the narrow alley and steep stone steps hid a womb of warmth and earth. Don Cayo and Teresa welcomed us, stools offered, drinks poured. Clara asked about the toad:

"Why here?"

"Ukhu Pacha," he said, lighting his cigarette. "The underworld, earth's womb. She guards abundance and fortune, born from the deep."

Behind the bar, a sign read: todo en vino, nada en vano — all in wine, nothing in vain. On the walls, murals of loyal friends, the family of the night.

That night, Clara danced like a spinning top: I got dizzy.

Don Cayo played the "gusano", an

old bandoneon, while Teresa's poetry fluttered like candle smoke.

Here, the toad is no mere beast. It is Pachamama's child, born from death's dark entrails, crossing from Manqha Pacha—the world beneath—to Kay Pacha, the world of dust and flesh, heralding rains, blessing the soil, promising fertility and fortune.

Installed on an altar, draped in serpentine blessings, offered copas, coca leaves, and Astoria cigarettes, the toad's silence was never empty again. Visitors knew the rite: ch'allar and light a cigarette to the stone lips—some to beg, some to confide, some simply to honour the unyielding stillness.

The Tavern's doors closed a long time ago, but the memory lingers—of lips pressed to stone, of coca and alcohol offerings, of the bride dressed in white spinning a cueca with the night.

Now, the toad rests proud and colossal on the bar of a hidden Trovería on Bolívar Street, near Plaza Murillo, its new altar.

Once more, drums roll through the old city streets; the toad dances with moceñada and aguayos, a floral colossus inviting and defying the rain, visiting old haunts, walking among ghosts.

Outside, La Paz weeps rain once more, don Cayo is gone, but through the great toad he still dances and celebrates beneath the storm.

No one ever tells you that the Green Cross breathes. That at night, when the wind shifts just slightly, the iron groans like a tired lung. The whole house exhales a chill that smells faintly of lime, burnt feathers, and the residue of an old confession. The walls—

thick as the guilt of centuries—sweat
minerals at dawn, trickling a pale green
moisture that locals wipe away without
comment, as though the house were an
elderly relative spitting up memories.

The invisible become impatient here.
Whatever they are by day—shadows, drafts,
uneasy sleep—at night they gather mass.
They become presences. They press against
the stone as if trying to seep through. They
lean into corners. They slip into cracks. They
whisper in Quechua, Aymara, Spanish, and in
the language of breath itself. And if you walk
by too fast, they cling to your ankles like cold
weeds.

The House of the Green Cross sits on
that crooked corner the way a heart sits in a
chest: beating, necessary, slightly diseased. A
stone relic, yes—but also a hinge. A hinge
between things that want to be forgotten and

things that refuse to die.

By the time Bocaisapo opened in its belly, the house had already collected more stories than any historian could bear to hear. The earth beneath it was already humming with the weight of unspoken years. Yet the tavern did not disturb the ghosts. It warmed them, fed them. They drifted through the cellar like old regulars returning to their favourite haunt.

When the toad arrived—stone, squat, dense with an old Andean sorrow—the house shifted. Something unlocked. It was as if the toad recognised the place, exhaling with relief, settling into the shadows as though crawling back into its original womb.

People say the toad chose the tavern, not the other way around.

The first nights were thick with omens. The lights flickered in patterns no electrician could decipher—soft Morse code tapped by unseen fingertips. The wooden beams cracked like bones adjusting themselves. Sometimes the air would tighten and hum, and everyone fell silent, even mid-drink, overcome by the sense that the room was taking a long, slow breath.

And the toad always watched. Stone eyes unblinking. Mouth slit open, forever ready to smoke.

Don Cayo believed the toad drank the music. His bandoneon's wheezing notes would slither into the stone, disappear, and then echo faintly hours later—deep, elongated, as if played by something subterranean. Teresa's poems soaked into its surface like spilled wine. Children swore they heard chewing noises at dawn, as though the toad were eating the darkness that pooled overnight.

The bar thrived because the toad remembered what abundance felt like. It had known deep, wet earth. It had felt the rumble of storms in its belly. It had been carved in the image of fertility, of rain, of the world that moves beneath our feet. When people danced, the toad grew warm. When people cried, the room shifted slightly—tilting toward them—listening.

But when fortune waned, the air around the toad thickened. A thin smell of damp clay began to rise from its base. Its stone grew darker, as if soaking up a sadness too heavy to carry. Don Cayo grew restless. He argued with shadows. He wept into his beers. He drank until dawn, his voice cracking as he recited promises he barely remembered making.

He had asked the toad for abundance. The toad had asked for sky.

It was an old imbalance, an ancient negotiation. The earth wants to rise. The living want to bury everything. A toad placed indoors begins to hunger for horizons, and hunger—when trapped—turns to sorrow.

When the Guild of the Toad began its annual processions, the city felt the shift. The idol was carried like a relic, but also like a prisoner briefly granted parole. Drums cracked the air. Torches hissed in the rain. People danced with the fervour of the half-possessed. The toad moved through the streets, absorbing the wet, absorbing the chants, absorbing the city's breath like a sponge swollen with centuries.

Some years, the rain followed the procession from start to finish, as if honoring an old pact. Other years, the sky held itself taut, waiting. But the toad always returned different—heavier,   lighter,   darker, brighter—wearing the weather like a new skin.

The night Clara danced for the first time in Bocaisapo, the whole room tilted. I swear the floor dipped slightly toward her, just as a lake dips when a storm approaches. Her spinning body pulled the air into a small vortex; even the toad seemed to shift its gaze, as though remembering something from a forgotten era when women danced in caves lit by animal fat and bone fire.

After that night, Clara claimed she could hear the toad breathe.

"Not with lungs," she insisted. "With weight."

She wasn't wrong. The bar grew heavier the longer one stayed. Chairs sank a millimetre deeper into the earth. Bottles on the shelves tilted infinitesimally toward the idol. And sometimes, late—very late—the candles flickered sideways, as though someone were inhaling them.

When Bocaisapo finally closed, the night recoiled. The alley grew thinner, like a ghost losing mass. The Green Cross dimmed. Even the phantoms seemed confused, pacing the steps as if searching for a missing limb.

Moving the toad was like moving a mountain.

It sighed once again when placed on its new altar, the way a tired traveller sighs when finally recognising home. Now it rests among poets, guitar players, bitter lovers, men with cracked voices—its new tribe. And those who visit know that to sit near it is to feel the weight of a wet earth pressing upward, gently, insistently.

When it dances in the rain—carried by hands older than their own bodies—it seems to swell, growing rounder, fuller, almost breathing. The drums speak to it. The aguayos wrap it like ceremonial skin. Children throw petals as though feeding a living creature.

And through it all, you can feel Don Cayo's laughter still—raw, hoarse, echoing somewhere between thunder and memory.

La Paz weeps. The streets rumble. The ghosts on Jaén Street blink awake.

And the toad, eternal wanderer, eternal watcher, keeps dancing through the red night. Lifting the dead with each step, reminding the living how close they stand to the soft, trembling edge between worlds.

Translucent

My name is Carlos, or at least that's what my parents called me.

But that was a long time ago, in a time that now feels like someone else's memory.

A photograph exposed to too much light.

Faces melted into pale smears.

Sometimes I wonder whether Carlos ever existed at all, or if he was just an early draft.

A trembling sketch made by hands that did not yet understand their own hunger.

Clara first emerged as an intuition, a flicker, a fragile gleam—

the thinnest membrane of light

trembling behind my eyelids.

She appeared the way a ghost appears: not suddenly,

but as a weight in the room, a coolness on the spine,

a breath that is not yours but knows your name.

And then, little by little, she pressed against me; she pressed against the walls of my chest, my throat, my face.

She pressed until the bone itself gave way.

She took shape, like fog deciding to become a person. And I retreated into the hollow.

A small chamber, damp, pulsating, without corners, a secret that throbbed between her ribs.

I was absorbed. Submerged.

Now I am only a quiet vibration hiding somewhere deep in the skull,

under her long hair, clinging like a forgotten nerve.

In the shower, the water fell like knives, and Clara's hand drew the razor along our skin.

The legs were bared, the hair dissolved.

Sacrifices to some nameless deity of water and metal.

The foam ran pink along the tiles.

I, meanwhile, suffocated in the steam.

I drowned, but it was not death, nor was it pleasure—it was something beyond both, a descent without name.

A descent into a place where language has no foothold.

A place where the self unravels quietly, strand by strand.

When I see her in the mirror, she looks at me as though I were the intruder, as though her face had hosted me long enough, and now demanded solitude.

And yet, today, there is nothing to see.

Carlos does not exist.

Not even a trace.

Clara speaks, Clara laughs, Clara drinks, Clara moves her body through the night. And I, immobile, am only a silence gnawing from within.

We wander the cemeteries. The niches are small doors awaiting us, dark cavities calling with a patience only the earth possesses.

From there, the city appears in its immensity, as if seen from the other side, not as a place, but as an organism, as if seen from the other side of the eyelid of the dead.

Sometimes I am convinced: I died long ago.

What moves in Clara is not her, not me, only the residue of a death that will not finish.

*

La Paz is not a city… it's a wound.

A crater torn into the flesh of the plateau, a gash still bleeding, pulsing.

The wind licks its edges. The fog settles in its depths like a bandage soaked in old tears.

The streets are veins. The neighbourhoods cling like crusts, pressed against ravines that gape like mouths.

Here, to live is to climb, to claw upward, to grow like a root lost in stone, desperately looking for water.

Perceived from above, the barrios exhale sound, the panting of brass bands, the thin wail of panpipes. The rattles of cans rolled by stray dogs: all stitched together by the uneven heartbeat of the city.

They also blow out aromas, meat burned to ash, fat dripping into fire, garlic and cumin twisting into steam.

La Paz exhales and inhales, exhales and inhales, and whoever listens too closely begins to hear the voice of something immense, the voice of the wound itself groaning in our lungs.

On Fridays, we rise into the orange cable car cabins, which are lanterns, coffins of glass suspended in air.

They drift above the houses with the gentleness of funeral boats. Below us, prayers curl upwards in thin threads.

Rosemary burns in tin cans, offering smoke that curls like a hand reaching upward, touching nothing, returning to nothing.

We glide low over Cementerio 'Llamita.'

The tombs of infants are so close we can almost touch them, as if caressing the face of unfinished lives.

The children's toys are scattered on the ground, faded plastic horses, cracked rattles, waiting for someone who will never return to play.

I shiver.

Clara smiles.

She murmurs: they are the blessed ones. And perhaps she is right.

Perhaps the fortunate are those who never learned how heavy it is to breathe.

*

At night, the city reveals her nakedness...

wrinkled concrete, cracked skin,

tangled wire scars in the hills, and she

is not a city

but ancient flesh held together

by stitches

the stitches of bones and the stitches

of blood

of those buried beneath the houses

and if

those bones were pulled away

she would unravel

she would scatter into

dust, into ash,

into silence.

The night thickened around us, folding streets over themselves like origami made from black velvet. Clara moved ahead, a sliver of light, and I drifted within, a pulse beneath her ribs, a vibration she didn't know she carried. The city whispered in tongues only half remembered; shadows clicking against stone, windows sighing, rooftops groaning with the weight of years.

We entered a barrio where the houses leaned like tired dancers, their wooden beams slick with rain and age. The walls exhaled heat, smoke, the memory of sweat and alcohol and burnt paper. I felt her step in rhythm with the city's heart, and in that rhythm, I knew: she was no longer Clara alone. She had become the body of La Paz walking.

In a courtyard, the air shimmered with dust motes and incense from a distant shrine. A single candle trembled on the windowsill. The light traced the edges of the wires overhead, and suddenly, I saw it: the city breathing through her. Every footfall pressed a vein into the streets, every hair-strand a filament in the mountains. She was both passenger and landscape, navigator and plateau, and I was the echo trapped beneath her skin.

We paused beside a fountain which had been dry for decades. Water stains ran like old tears. Clara touched the cracked stone, and the wall pulsed back. I realised then: the city had learned her name. The bricks whispered it in sequence, and the rusted pipes answered with hollow laughter. I tried to speak, but my words dissolved into fog. I existed only as the memory of sound, a phantom vibration following her in silence.

At the edge of a cemetery, the fog thickened until the tombs became skeletons of hills. The toys scattered on the ground, forgotten and brittle, began to twitch, rearranging themselves in impossible patterns. Clara knelt among them. Her hands hovered over a cracked rattle, a miniature horse, a tin soldier. They answered her touch with tremors. The dead were not asleep—they were remembering her.

And I—still vibrating somewhere beneath her hair—felt the city tighten around us. The plateaus pressed in, the ravines whispered into our chest, the wind carried the scent of earth and ash and iron. We were suspended between the living and the buried, the past and the breath of now.

She laughed. It was not a sound so much as an unfolding of light, a resonance with stone and air. The cable cars sang overhead in deep orange tones, and the city itself seemed to rise to meet her, street by street, alley by alley. Even the stray dogs paused, noses raised, listening.

Somewhere far away, a bell tolled. Or maybe it was the echo of a child's toy, a metal horse falling into a drain. Time bled sideways. We walked, and the city unstitched itself beneath our feet. Houses unlatched doors, walls leaned closer, the fog gathered into her silhouette. Clara had become the fissure, the wound, the living echo of La Paz itself.

I wanted to warn her, to call her back. But no sound would leave me. I am a shadow she carries, a silent heartbeat, a whisper she can't hear but that anchors her to my ghost.

And still, I follow, through cemeteries, empty markets, streets folding like old envelopes, tracing her steps in a city that remembers every fragment of our skin.

The plateau waits. The plateau watches. And we—Clara and I, or what is left of me—wander inside its wound, carried on its breath, swallowed in its pulse, unnamed, unspeaking, unending.

Acknowledgments

I thank Noble Legacy for their editorial work. I would like to thank my children, Mila Araoz Ellis, Mati Araoz Ellis, and Nico Denvir Araoz, as well as my brothers, Luis Araoz S. and Mauricio Araoz S. for their constant support.

Several people have offered valuable advice at different stages of the writing process. I thank Griet Scheldeman, Maialen Galarraga, Hugh Tuffen, Rebecca Ellis, Eleanor Denvir, Alison Kaberry, Anastasja Katzinova, and Milan MA Gonzales.

I am especially grateful to Carlo Matthews for his extremely valuable advice and generous editorial support, and for keeping the laughter alive.

About the Author

Gonzalo Araoz is a professional anthropologist and a self-taught artist. His visual and written work is shaped largely through bricolage—not merely a method, but a way of inhabiting the world. He gathers remnants, discarded objects, images stripped of their original destinies, and grants them new resonances.

This practice, born from recycling what the world abandons at its margins, became for him a way of tracing origins and imagining futures. For him, perception is neither singular nor still. Araoz remains attentive to the ways in which sensations overlap—how an image may carry a sound, how an aroma may awaken a memory, how the senses intertwine to form unexpected encounters.

Endless possibilities arise. Some take shape in his anthropological and fictional writings; others find expression in his visual work; and others linger in silence, suspended, waiting for the moment when they too may emerge

Published in Collaboration with Noble
Legacy Publishing
www.noblelegacypublishing.co.uk